This book
belongs to

The Nome King's Shadow in OZ

THE NOME KING'S SHADOW IN OZ

By

Gilbert M. Sprague

Illustrated by Donald Abbott

NEW YORK

The Emerald City Press

To Jennifer

The first person who ever told me
to write a story for fun.

– G.M.S.

The Nome King's Shadow in Oz

Text Copyright © 1992 by Gilbert M. Sprague
Illustrations Copyright © 1992 by Donald Abbott

Printed in the U.S.A.

The Emerald City Press
A Division Of
Books of Wonder
132 Seventh Avenue
New York, NY 10011

ISBN 0-929605-37-3 (paperback)

2 3 4 5 6 7 8 9

TABLE OF CONTENTS

The Nome King's Shadow

One day, Princess Ozma and a lot of her friends were visiting the strange and fascinating countries on the other side of the Deadly Desert surrounding Oz. While they were there, they were joined by Dorothy Gale of Kansas, who had been ship-wrecked during a terrible storm at sea and had washed ashore in these strange lands. Together, they came to the kingdom of the Nomes, a vast realm of tunnels, caverns, and caves deep beneath the surface of the earth.

Even though Ozma and her friends arrived as the Nome King's guests, he took them prisoner and magically turned them into bric-a-brac ornaments. For a while, it looked like they were going to stay that way forever.

Luckily for everyone (except the Nomes) Dorothy had brought along a brave hen named Billina. Billina stayed out of the Nome King's clutches, found the secret to his magic spell and helped free Ozma, Dorothy, their friends and all the Nome King's other prisoner's, too.

Billina was able to avoid capture because hen eggs are poisonous to Nomes, and so the Nomes were deathly afraid of Billina. The Nome King was so frightened when he saw Billina that he fell to pieces.

When he pulled himself back together, he forgot all about his shadow, which had scurried behind his throne. There it hid, a dark form with jagged, upstanding locks of hair on top of its long, thin head, a big, round belly and short, spindly legs.

The Nome King fled from his throne room, leaving his shadow behind. By the time he looked, he had grown a new one, so he never missed his old one.

The Nome King's old shadow hid behind the throne while Billina and Ozma's other friends defeated the Nome King's armies.

"Even though my master's troops run away in fear, all is not lost," the Nome King's shadow said to himself from the safety of his hiding place. "I am still here to make mischief and avenge the Nome King. No one, not even that dratted hen, can harm me, for I am a shadow, not a Nome. And no one can harm a shadow! I will follow Ozma and her people back to their homes in the

The Nome King's Shadow

Emerald City and there I will do something so terrible and so wicked that all Oz will quake in fear. From this day on I shall be Shady, the Mighty Apparition, Avenger of the Nome King's honor..."

Shady was so awestruck by this brash speech that he suddenly felt shy.

"Well," he went on, "at least I'll get even with the hen."

After the battle was over Ozma, her friends and all the other people Billina had rescued left the land of the Nomes. Lickety-split, Shady flitted out from behind the throne and followed them.

As they went along, Shady imagined he was chasing Ozma and all her friends, especially Billina. He imagined that they were terrified of him and were running away as fast as they could. It never occurred to him that he was acting just like a shadow by following in their footsteps.

Shady's daydreams were dashed when they came to the end of the tunnel. Brilliant sunlight streamed through the entrance. Dorothy let out a tinkling cry of joy. Ozma laughed at the sight of the light. Everyone in the party surged forward, with Shady right at their heels.

An everyday shadow cannot exist if there is

The Nome King's Shadow in Oz

nothing to cast it. Shady, being a magical shadow, was free to come and go as he pleased. Even so, he could not survive in bright light. The dark nooks and dimly lit hallways of the Nome King's domain were a perfect home for him.

When Shady reached the end of the tunnel, the sunlight burned him. If he ventured any further out, the sun would bleach him right out of existence. It turned out Shady was wrong. There was one thing that *could* harm a shadow.

Shady pulled himself back into the tunnel and watched while the people from Oz ran on ahead without him. Bitter frustration welled up in his shadowy heart.

To make matters worse, Billina turned around, scratched the ground, bobbed her head and clucked in a most insulting way. That was her way of letting the Nome King know she was glad to be out of his clutches. But, to Shady, it seemed as if she knew he was there and was laughing at him. All he could do was shake his fists and stamp his feet in frustration.

Nightfall brought darkness and safety. Shady glided out of the tunnel. A brisk, fresh breeze was blowing. In all the days he belonged to the Nome King, Shady had never been outside. This was the first breeze he ever felt. It felt so good, he spread out his arms and let the cool air flow through him.

"The world must be quite a magnificent place if there are things like this in it," Shady said to himself. For a moment, he lost himself. Then the breeze died. "But I have a score to settle!" he snapped.

Shady looked around and soon he spied the tracks left by Ozma and her friends. He set off after the people from Oz.

Try as he could, Shady was not able to catch up with Ozma and her friends. Shady was used to following his master everywhere without having to think. Now that he was on his own, he had to make a decision every single time he moved. Making all these decisions by himself slowed him down.

Being a shadow, he didn't have to worry about tripping over roots or bumping into tree trunks. Even so, he had to watch where he was going very carefully, just to make sure he stayed on the same path as the people from Oz.

Dawn was just beginning to break when Shady left the woods. The path crossed a field of broken boulders. Keeping to the shade of the giant rocks, the Nome King's shadow flitted along. As the sun grew stronger, Shady grew weaker and he still saw no sign of the people from Oz.

He turned a sharp corner. There, the path ended at the poisonous sands of the Deadly Desert. In days gone by, Shady had heard the Nome King and his advisors talking about this desolate wasteland, so he recognized it the instant he saw it.

Even though Shady knew the sands would not harm him since he was a shadow, the sight of the bright sun beating down on the desert struck terror in his heart. To make matters worse, he saw Dorothy and Ozma and all the other people from Oz off in the distance, walking across the desert. A thick carpet covered the deadly sands beneath their feet. The carpet unrolled in front of them and rolled up again behind them as they walked.

Shady's plan to capture Ozma and her friends was ruined. There was no shelter from the sun for as far as the eye could see. Shady stood in the shadow of the last boulder at the edge of the desert, jumped up and down, stamped his feet, shook his fists in the air and swore.

"Whatever shall I do?" Shady cried. "I have such a powerful urge to be wicked, but now I'll never be able to act on it. It just isn't fair!"

As the people from Oz disappeared from view, Shady sank to the ground and went into a first class sulk.

The Royal Hen of Oz

While Shady sulked, Princess Ozma and her friends went on their merry way to the Emerald City.

Crowds of cheering people met the travelers at the city gates. A parade, complete with brass bands and confetti, sprang up as Princess Ozma, Dorothy Gale and the rest of the exalted heroes marched through the streets.

The loudest cheers of all greeted Billina. News of the brave hen's deeds had spread like wildfire among Princess Ozma's loyal citizens and they were all eager to catch a glimpse of this newest addition to Princess Ozma's wide assortment of wonderful friends. As Billina passed, the people of the Emerald City poured out their thanks to her.

"Praise your feathers!" cried some.

"Welcome to the chicken who's no chicken!" cried others.

But more and more often, the people cried, "Long live the Royal Hen of Oz!"

Billina strutted along, her head bobbing up and down and her feathers puffed up in pride. From time to time she flew up and circled above the adoring crowd, clucking out her thanks for their heartfelt reception.

Days of feasting, dancing, merrymaking and joy followed the triumphant return of Princess Ozma and her friends.

When the time finally came for Dorothy to return to her Uncle Henry, Billina said, "I should like to stay here in Oz. I can talk here, but not back home. The people here are especially kind to chickens. Furthermore, the bugs and ants I've found to eat here are the finest I've ever had anywhere. Therefore, I shall stay in Oz, if Princess Ozma will have me."

"Of course we'll have you!" said Ozma.

Once Dorothy had been sent on her way by means of magic, Ozma said to Billina, "Now that you have made your decision to stay with us, I will show you our gratitude by building you the finest chicken coop anywhere in the world."

Over the next several days, workmen bustled about a sunny lawn on the grounds of the Royal Palace. They erected a wooden coop painted bright yellow with green trim. Its roof rose to a sharp point, topped with a crossbar of horizontal perches which pointed north, south, east and west.

Outside the front door of the coop, Ozma's workers built a beautiful, bubbling, splashing fountain.

Day by day Billina watched as this palatial residence was built. When Billina's new home was finished, the Scarecrow paid her a visit.

"Hello my fine-feathered friend," said the Scarecrow.

"Hello my smiling-faced friend," said Billina. "To what do I owe the honor of your company?"

"The honor is all mine," said the Scarecrow. "Now that you have a magnificent, new home you are going to need to furnish it."

"That is true," said Billina.

"As far as I can tell," said the Scarecrow, "the best furnishing for a hen as noble as you is soft, fresh straw to line your nesting box and all the other parts of your home."

"That is *exactly* what I was thinking of!" said Billina.

"Excellent," said the Scarecrow. "You have, standing before you, the foremost expert on straw in all of Oz. Texture, consistency, aroma, pliability, thickness and durability — I know it all! I have come to offer you my assistance."

"How wise of you to think that I would need your advice now that it is time for me to furnish

my home!" said Billina.

The Scarecrow doffed his hat. "It is a pleasure to be at your service," he said.

Together, Billina and the Scarecrow went to the farmer's market in one of the Emerald City's great squares. There, the Scarecrow helped Billina pick out the finest, sweetest smelling straw she had ever seen.

The farmer was so proud to be visited by two such renowned celebrities that he had his son carry the bales back to the Royal Palace.

The farmer's son gaped in wonder as the Scarecrow replaced the stuffing in his legs and Billina lined her new home.

When they were done and the farmer's son had gone on his way, Billina and the Scarecrow sat in the sun talking. As they chatted, Billina spied an ant crawling by and snapped it up.

"Do you like the way ants taste?" asked the Scarecrow.

"Very much," replied Billina.

"What do you do if you don't find enough ants and bugs?" asked the Scarecrow.

"Then I go hungry," replied Billina.

"Have you ever thought of adding corn to your diet?" asked the Scarecrow.

"I have always found corn to be tough and starchy, without much flavor at all," said Billina.

"I have seen an ear or two of corn grow in my day," said the Scarecrow. "You must not have been fed the right corn if you did not find it sweet and succulent."

"If you truly believe that," said Billina, "then I shall have to try some."

"I will have a bucketful spread on the ground for you tomorrow," said the Scarecrow.

True to the Scarecrow's word, a bucketful of the sweetest, tenderest, most succulent corn Billina had ever tasted arrived at her front door the next day. When Billina expressed her thanks, the Scarecrow promised that corn would be served to her that same way every morning.

Now that Billina was content and settled into her luxurious new home, she began to lay egg after egg. After sitting on them for some time, a thriving brood of little chicks hatched out.

Billina named all the girl chicks Dorothy in honor of the girl who had brought her to Oz and made all her joy possible. Just to help keep things straight, Billina named all her boy chicks Daniel.

Shortly after the chicks hatched, the Scarecrow paid Billina a visit.

"Isn't it confusing to call them all either Dorothy or Daniel?" he asked.

"Oh, no!" said Billina. "Think how complicated it would be to give each one of them a different name! How would I ever be able to remember who was who?"

The Scarecrow was preparing to answer Billina's question when he looked at the brood of identical chicks bobbing about her feet. Words failed him and he nodded at Billina's great wisdom.

Across the Deadly Desert

Meanwhile, Shady sat at the edge of the Deadly Desert, sulking the days away.

Shady kept thinking things like, "They've gone and I'll never have the chance to terrorize them again. How can fate be so cruel to a shadow wronged?" and, "I'm just a helpless shadow, lost in the big, bright world and in constant danger of being burned away to nothingness. How can anyone as weak and defenseless as me ever hope to avenge himself when the whole world is against him?"

After a month or so, Shady began to get tired of doing nothing. Before he could stop himself he found himself thinking, "Nothing will stand in the way of the Mighty Shady, Avenger of the Nome King!" He tried to go back to sulking, but it just wasn't as much fun.

A few weeks later, Shady began to wonder, "How *am* I going to get to Oz?"

That night, Shady got up to take a look around.

"If I want to get to Oz, I have to cross the desert without the sun hurting me," he thought,

Across the Deadly Desert

"but there isn't any shelter from the sun for the whole expanse of the desert."

Shady floated out onto the sands, then darted back. "Most shadows don't have to worry about the sun," he thought, "because they have a master to protect them. They pay for their safety by sacrificing their freedom. I am free but not safe, therefore I need to find something to keep me safe that does not take away my freedom! Let's see what I can do with the boulder I've been using."

Shady sailed back to where he had been sitting and tried to pick up the boulder. It would not budge, but this did not discourage him.

"Wouldn't I make a foolish sight, carrying a boulder for miles and miles," he thought. "I need something more portable..." And, in a flash, Shady knew exactly what he needed. "An umbrella!" he shouted with joy.

Quick as a wink, Shady soared up the path back into the woods and found a long, thin stick that had fallen from a tree. Snap, snap, snap he broke off all the twigs, leaving the stick smooth. Rustle, rustle, snip, snip he pulled down six broad, green leaves from a spreading bush. With a twist and a bend, with a spin and a knot, Shady used a twining vine to bind the leaves together in a handsome, spreading crown. By twisting another length of vine in a tightly wrapped spiral, he fastened the crown of leaves onto the end of the long, thin stick.

The sun was just beginning to rise when he finished his umbrella. He held it up and the broad, green leaves cast a protective shadow over him.

Capering and cavorting, Shady pranced down out of the woods, past the broken boulders and out onto the sands of the Deadly Desert.

The Deadly Desert is vast. The Deadly Desert is wide. Being made only out of shadow, the trip across the Deadly Desert did not tire Shady out nor did it make him thirsty. Holding his umbrella over his head as he went, Shady sailed over roasting dunes and soared over baking plains. He chuckled to himself for having cheated the sun, praised himself for his cleverness and let his imagination run wild with thoughts of terrorizing Ozma and her friends.

Shady may have been made from only shadow so the sun's scorching heat did not bother him in the least, but his umbrella was not made from shadow at all. Shady's umbrella, his only precious shelter against the sun's brilliant light, was made

Across the Deadly Desert

out of fresh, moist leaves. As the blazing sun beat down on the umbrella, the leaves began to dry out. As the leaves began to dry out, they began to shrivel and crack, letting tiny beams of sunlight in. The sunlight stung Shady and he pulled himself into a tight little ball of darkness and huddled under the darkest part of the umbrella. A race was on to see which would last longer, the blazing sunlight or Shady's umbrella.

The umbrella won and, with the fall of night, Shady heaved a great sigh of relief and surged forward, twice as fast as before.

A silvery moon rose, casting cool, enchanting light over the barren waste. Shady revelled in the moonlight. It reminded him of the soothing light cast by the cold, hard jewels in the Nome King's underground realm.

By moving as fast as he possibly could, Shady crossed the Desert as quickly as Dorothy had when she had traveled by cyclone on her very first trip to Oz.

Just as the first light was breaking in the east, Shady reached the edge of the lush, green fields of Oz.

"Yahoo-ooey!" he yodelled in glee. "Tremble all you people of Oz. Shady the Mighty Apparition is here!" Shady cried. He was so excited, he soared up into the air. He somersaulted high in the sky and streaked back down to earth, whooping as he came.

The dried and brittle leaves of the umbrella crumbled and broke from the force of Shady's descent. The bright day was dawning and all Shady had for protection was a stick. But Shady did not panic. He looked at the stick in his hand and laughed.

The orange and red light swelled in the east. Shady scanned the horizon for shelter. In the distance he saw a line of trees. Without so much as a moment's hesitation, he set out for the trees at top speed.

Shady dived into the cool, green shadows just as the sun poked its sleepy head up over the horizon and a host of birds burst into a joyous chorus of song.

Shadow Magic

Shady drifted lazily to a stop and sat down at the base of a spreading pine tree. He felt something in his hand and looked down. To his surprise, he was still holding the useless stick from his umbrella.

"I thought I'd dropped you, my friend," Shady said to the stick. He opened his hand and tried to let go of it, but the stick was stuck to his palm.

"I appreciate your loyalty," Shady said, "But you have outlasted your usefulness to me." He shook his hand, but still the stick remained stuck to his palm. He took hold of it with his other hand and tried to pull it loose. That hurt, but the stick still did not come loose.

"You are stuck to me as a shadow sticks to his master!" Shady said.

Shady sat bolt upright in surprise. "As a shadow sticks to his master...," he muttered.

Shady bent over his hand, peering with fascination at the place where the stick and his hand came together. He could see little hooks growing out of the palm of his hand. The hooks were sunk into the stick, holding it firmly in place.

"Well, what do you know?" said Shady. "Shadow hooks! Who ever heard of such a thing? This must be how a shadow keeps such a tight hold on his master. I must have grown them as an involuntary reaction!"

Shady twisted the stick from side to side, trying to loosen the shadow hooks. At first the stick would not budge and his hand hurt like the dickens. Slowly, by trial and error, Shady found that by twisting the stick just so and twisting his hand just so in a very different way he could unhook the shadow hooks.

Now, I am not going to tell you precisely how Shady did this, because if you try this, your own shadow might accidently get loose and who knows what kind of trouble it might cause!

As Shady's shadow hooks came loose, he saw exactly how they held shadow and master locked together. He saw how the master's movements flowed through the shadow hooks, pulling the shadow this way and that, always keeping it safe from the sun and other bright lights.

"Isn't it amazing how, just when you think you

know everything, you find out something new?" Shady said as he let the stick fall to the ground.

Immediately, Shady began testing his new discovery. First, he unhooked the shadow of the tree he was sheltering under and hooked himself on.

As soon as he unhooked the tree's natural shadow, it started to drift off. He had to grab it so that it wouldn't float into the sunlight and burn away to nothing, leaving him hooked to the tree and unable to free himself until nightfall. After a few minutes, Shady unhooked himself from the tree and reattached its natural shadow.

"Now I wonder if I can reverse the usual flow, and use the shadow hooks to control the former master," said Shady. With a quick twist he hooked himself back onto the tree. After a few moments of intense concentration, he found that he could indeed use the shadow hooks to shake the branches of the tree back and forth, exactly as if they were tossing in the wind.

Pride filled Shady's dark heart. "Now I can sneak up on an unsuspecting beast, unhook its shadow, hook myself to it and force it to do my bidding by twisting my shadow hooks this way and that. The beast will provide me with vital protection from the sun and give me both camouflage from my enemies and a tool with which to wreak havoc. I will get to the Emerald City yet, and make Princess Ozma's people, especially that dratted hen, quake in terror!"

Shady was so taken with his new plot that he capered up and down, chortling and giggling. After a few moments, he got control of himself.

"Now," he shrieked, "I'm off to find a victim to aid me in my fiendish quest!"

The Shadow Lengthens

Shady's natural instinct for darkness took him deeper into the forest. Mighty trees with massive trunks towered over him. Their leafy, spreading branches shut out nearly all the light. Although the sun shone brightly overhead, the forest floor was sunk in a dim, green twilight.

Shady did not have any clear idea what kind of beast he was looking for. His only thought was to capture something BIG.

He went deeper and deeper into the woods without encountering so much as a squirrel much less anything big. The afternoon shadows were growing long and Shady's temper was growing short when he heard two growly voices coming through the trees.

Shady moved towards them until a great roar rang out, freezing him in his tracks. The roar quieted back down to words.

"I really wish you wouldn't talk that way, my friend," it said.

"How can I possibly talk any other way?" said the other growly voice. "I would need to have a different voice if I were to talk another way, and I only have one."

"You misunderstand me," said the first growler. "I have no quarrel with your voice. What I meant was, I wish you would pick a different topic of conversation."

"I'm sorry if my discussing the culinary ecstasy of devouring succulent babies disturbs you," said the second voice, "but I find that whenever I am idle, I am unable to think about anything else."

During this conversation Shady glided closer and closer to the voices. They sounded familiar to him and, when the speakers came into view, he saw why.

The owner of the first voice was a tremendous lion with tawny fur. His whole head was crowned with a mane that glowed like a halo. The second speaker was a gigantic tiger with orange fur, slashed with jet black stripes.

These two spectacular cats were none other than Princess Ozma's friends, the Cowardly Lion and the Hungry Tiger. They sat together beside a babbling brook. Shady recognized them instantly, for they had accompanied Ozma and her friends on her journey to the land of the Nomes.

"What remarkable luck!" chortled Shady to

himself. "One of these beasts will provide me with the ideal camouflage for making mischief in Princess Ozma's court. Just think of it! If I were to take hold of one of these beasts, I could devour that dratted hen in one gulp, feathers and all!"

"If you only think of eating babies when you are idle," said the Cowardly Lion, "then perhaps it is best if we started back to the Emerald City as our work here is done."

"I'm not ready to start back yet, my friend," said the Hungry Tiger. "Princess Ozma did not ask us to hurry, and I am enjoying this moment of quiet. However, if you insist, I will keep my carnivorous thoughts to myself so as not to bruise your delicate sensibilities any more."

The Hungry Tiger let out a huge yawn, showing what seemed to be thousands of jagged teeth. Then, his head fell to his paws and his eyes slid closed.

"That will be fine," said the Cowardly Lion. He, too, rested his head on his paws. In a matter of moments, both cats were fast asleep.

"Now is my golden opportunity," chortled Shady. "This is a better chance than I ever could have hoped for! The lion, who has a much gentler disposition, will be the better target for me."

The Shadow Lengthens

He glided slyly across the brook and slipped around behind the sleeping cats. Once in position behind the Cowardly Lion, Shady carefully measured the length of the Lion's shadow. He set sights on the place where the shadow hooks held the big cat and its shadow together.

Shady's heart pounded as he closed in on the Cowardly Lion.

Suddenly, a dark form rose up in front of Shady. "Hey!" it said, "What's going on here?"

Shady was so startled it was all he could do to keep his wits about him.

"I was just coming over to enjoy the protection of this magnificent beast. I am, you see, a poor shadow who has lost his master and needs protection from the sun."

"Why didn't you ask first?" said the dark form.

"I didn't think anybody would mind," said Shady.

"I am this magnificent beast's shadow," said the dark form, "and I most certainly *do* mind, if I'm not asked politely!"

"I'm terribly sorry," said Shady, "But I don't believe you are this beast's shadow. After all, he is fast asleep and you are talking and moving about independently of him. Are you sure he ·is yours?"

"My master is the world-famous Cowardly Lion," said the Cowardly Lion's shadow. "When your master is as wary as mine, you develop your own sense of caution."

"I've never heard of anything like that!" said Shady, not thinking he had developed his own sense of mischief because he had started life as the Nome King's shadow.

"Haven't you ever heard of someone having eyes in back of their head?" asked the Cowardly Lion's shadow.

"Yes," said Shady.

"Well, that's what they mean!"

"Goodness," said Shady, adding sugar to his voice, "You are so wise! As I said, I'm a poor shadow left alone to wander the world without a master to protect me or guide me. Could I please join you and share the protection of the regal, noble, beloved and gentle Cowardly Lion?"

"I'm not sure," said the Cowardly Lion's shadow, "If I'm going to take you on board, I'll need to know who your original master was and how you happened to lose him."

"I have a very dark past," said Shady, putting on a pathetic tone, sliding closer and closer as he talked. "I'd rather not discuss it, because it upsets me so much."

"I'm sorry to pry," said the Cowardly Lion's shadow.

"That's quite all right," said Shady, snuffling with great gusto. He drifted past the Cowardly Lion's shadow towards the sleeping body of the great cat. "Surely you won't mind if I just rest here," he said.

"No, I don't mind," said the Cowardly Lion's shadow.

With a sigh, Shady settled down very close to where the shadow hooks held the Cowardly Lion's shadow in place. The Cowardly Lion's shadow thinned back down and stretched out on the grass behind his master. Shady waited a few minutes. Then, slowly and carefully, he slid his hand towards the shadow hooks. He took hold of one of them and began to twist it oh so very slowly.

"You ungrateful, wretched traitor!" roared the Cowardly Lion's shadow, rising up again and bearing down on Shady.

"Cower before me!" said Shady, unfastening the first shadow hook. "I am Shady, Avenger of the Nome King's honor and scourge of Oz!"

"Begone!" roared the Cowardly Lion's shadow,

swatting Shady with one of his paws.

Shady lost his grip on the shadow hooks and sailed through the air, landing in the branches of a nearby tree.

"And don't you dare come back!" The Cowardly Lion's shadow roared up the tree.

The fight between the shadows woke the two cats.

"What's all this noise?" asked the Hungry Tiger.

"Master!" said the Cowardly Lion's shadow, "A shadowy agent from the Nome King tried to take you away from me."

"Who is that talking?" asked the Cowardly Lion.

"I think it's your shadow!" said the Hungry Tiger.

"How curious!" said the Cowardly Lion. "This is the first time he's ever spoken to me."

"This is the first time I've ever needed to, you big ball of fur!" shouted his shadow. "We must go to the Emerald City at once to warn Princess Ozma of this danger from the land of the Nomes!"

Shady was so terrified that, without waiting another moment, he set off through the tree branches as fast as he could.

The Flight to the Emerald City

"The ground just isn't safe for me," thought Shady, "not with those wild cats on the loose." He swung from one branch to another as quickly as he could and still avoid the occasional patches of sun that broke through this high up.

Swinging in the branches was so much fun that Shady was soon over his fright. "Now that those brutes know I am here," Shady said to himself, as he dangled and bounced from a particularly springy branch, "I need to find another victim to take over. I need to reach the Emerald City and wreak havoc there while I still have the element of surprise on my side! Perhaps I can find a great bird nesting here in the forest eaves. A pair of mighty wings would certainly carry me to the Emerald City with great speed."

Much as he would rather have kept swinging madly about, Shady slowed his pace. As he went, he scanned the branches around him for nests. He did not have to look long at all. There, in a near-

36

by tree was a huge bird's nest.

Shady snuck up on the nest. Sure enough, a sharp-beaked hawk was sleeping there. But Shady faced a problem. There were no branches blocking the sun above the hawk's nest. Although this meant warm roosting for the hawk, for Shady, the sunlight meant certain destruction.

Shady nipped back into the green twilight below the nest.

"There has to be a way!" he said. "I haven't found the perfect tool for my wickedness and now not be able to use it!"

Even faster than he found the hawk's nest, Shady found the way to get to the hawk. The hawk's nest was made from sticks and there were lots of cracks between them. By making himself as thin as a ribbon, Shady was able to thread himself through the cracks and zig-zag his way up into the nest. Soon, he was resting comfortably in the dark underneath the hawk.

Shady's invasion was so smooth and gentle that neither the hawk nor his shadow woke up.

Working slowly and carefully, fighting the urge to panic and rush, Shady unhooked the hawk's natural shadow and hooked himself on.

"Up, Messenger of Doom!" Shady cried. He

jerked sharply on the shadow hooks. "The time has come for me launch my attack on the people of Oz!"

"Aiee!" cried the hawk as he awoke.

Shady pulled on the shadow hooks again, launching the hawk out of his nest. Fortunately, the hawk's natural shadow was as sharp-eyed, quick-witted and fast as his master. As the hawk rose out of the nest, his natural shadow grabbed onto Shady and rose up, too.

"Witches and wizards!" cried the hawk. He flapped his wings hard, trying to regain control of himself. "What fiendish fate has befallen me!"

"You are now the slave of the Mighty Shady, Scourge of Oz and Avenger of the Nome King!" Shady cried. He leaned against the shadow hooks with all his might and forced the hawk to turn towards the Emerald City.

Below him, the hawk's natural shadow swung part way out into the sunlight.

"Burning, blistering heat!" cried the hawk's natural shadow from below Shady. He rolled himself up in a tiny ball from the pain. This cut down on wind resistance and the big hawk shot forward at great speed.

"What's causing me all this nuisance?" said

The Flight to the Emerald City

Shady.

"I belong to Thunder Wing, the hawk you are stealing," said the hawk's shadow. "I'm not going to let you get away with this!"

"There is no stopping the Avenger of the Nome King!" Shady shrieked.

Shady tried without luck to kick Thunder Wing's shadow away. The shadow took so much of Shady's attention that, shrieking in anger, the hawk was able to turn away from the Emerald City, back towards his nest.

"Oh no you don't!" cried Shady. He pulled hard on the shadow hooks, turning the hawk back towards the Emerald City. But this momentary diversion was enough for Thunder Wing's shadow to tear at Shady some more, so Shady had to pay attention to the trouble below.

Thus Shady, Thunder Wing and the hawk's shadow looped and spiralled through the air, moving slowly closer and closer to the Emerald City, screeching and fighting as they went.

Hard as Thunder Wing and his shadow fought, Shady had the advantage. He was hooked onto Thunder Wing by shadow hooks. The hawk's shadow could only hang on for dear life and Thunder Wing had to obey Shady's commands.

Whenever the hawk's shadow climbed to a place where he could fight Shady, Shady made Thunder Wing veer. This exposed the poor shadow to the burning rays of the sun.

Thunder Wing had never, even in his worst nightmares, dreamed that he would have to fight a battle like this and had no idea what to do. No matter what, Shady stayed right behind him as only a shadow can. Slowly the pain of sunburn wore out the hawk's shadow and exhaustion wore out Thunder Wing. Eventually, they stopped fighting with Shady. With a cry of triumph, Shady pushed the hawk higher into the sky and set a straight course for the Emerald City.

Soon, the sun set. No longer afraid of being burned, the hawk's shadow renewed the fight. As he started to struggle, Thunder Wing felt new, painful tugging on the shadow hooks.

"Stop! I am losing strength and your fight will only tire me faster. We are so high up now that if I fall out of the sky, I will die!" cried Thunder Wing.

As night fell, Shady, the hawk and his shadow struck an uneasy truce and they flew on straight and true.

When morning dawned, Thunder Wing let out

a cry. Ahead rose the beautiful towers and mighty turrets of the Emerald City. Shady spied the towers and turrets as well.

"Fly on! Fly on!" he called, pushing Thunder Wing as hard as he could. "Shady, the Mighty Apparition has come, bringing doom to the Emerald City!"

"Oh, be quiet," snapped the hawk, stroking his wings up and down. But this just made Shady cackle wickedly.

Soon, Shady, the hawk and his shadow were flying over the Emerald City.

"Down!" commanded Shady, pulling on the shadow hooks.

But Thunder Wing did not begin to drop!

Once Thunder Wing and his shadow stopped fighting, the hawk had started to think. He felt exactly where Shady's shadow hooks held him. He concentrated very hard on that place and found that, although he could not completely resist Shady's control, he could fend it off for a little while. Rather than give this away, he came up with a plan to get rid of Shady and help save the Emerald City. He kept flying as Shady commanded, waiting for just the right moment to put his plan to work.

The Nome King's Shadow in Oz

With sure, strong strokes of his wings, the hawk flew straight for the highest tower of Princess Ozma's Royal Palace.

"You must obey the will of the Mighty Shady!" screamed Shady, pulling viciously on the shadow hooks.

Thunder Wing faltered in his course and his speed slowed, but by taking a deep breath, he was able to keep on flying. From below, his shadow felt the change and again began fighting Shady.

One, two, three, four strokes of the hawk's mighty wings and Thunder Wing crashed with a smash and a bash, right into the highest tower of Princess Ozma's Royal Palace.

Then, Shady and Thunder Wing and his shadow were spinning and falling down, down, down. It was all Shady and the hawk's shadow could do to stay out of the sun. It was all Thunder Wing could do to shake Shady loose without injuring himself or his shadow.

They all landed with a tremendous crash in the middle of a yard outside Princess Ozma's palace. The whole yard was full of tiny little chicks. They pecked away at kernels of corn spread on the ground. They took no notice of the hawk's sudden arrival.

The Flight to the Emerald City

The force of the landing tore Shady loose from Thunder Wing and sent him spinning. The morning sunlight was white hot heat to Shady. He grabbed the shelter of the first thing he spun past — one of the tiny little chicks. The chick was so wrapped up in finding kernels of corn, she didn't even notice the sudden substitution of Shady for her own shadow.

The hawk's shadow landed underneath Thunder Wing and quickly sank his shadow hooks back into the mighty bird. Thunder Wing was dazed and one of his wings was wrenched. He lay in the yard panting.

While Shady watched from the protection of the little chick, a stately yellow hen strutted up to Thunder Wing.

"Excuse me," she said to the hawk in an officious voice, "just what do you mean by dropping in on my family during our breakfast?"

Thunder Wing groaned.

"It's that dratted hen!" Shady said to himself as he watched the two birds talking. "I am now the proud owner of one of Billina's chicks. I shall cause all the mischief I can with this silly little thing. Surely, the trouble I cause will reflect badly on her mother!"

"What's happening?" peeped the little chick as Shady steered her out of the yard.

Thinking fast, Shady said, "Be quiet! I'm a messenger from Princess Ozma and I need your help with a secret mission."

"Oh, what fun!" said the chick as they entered Princess Ozma's palace.

A Warning Ignored

The morning Shady arrived in the Emerald City began very much like every other morning since Billina became a mother. Billina and her chicks were up with the sun and out eating the corn that had so kindly been spread for them.

As there is very little danger to small animals in the settled portions of Oz, none of the chicks paid any attention when the hawk raced overhead. Only Billina, who had been hatched and reared in Mortal Lands looked up. She was just in time to see the hawk fly straight into the highest tower of the palace.

"This is not good at all!" Billina clucked in surprise.

The royal hen of Oz watched as the hawk fell down, down, down and landed with a crash in her yard. She strutted right up to the hawk.

"Excuse me," she said. "Just what do you mean by dropping in on my family during our breakfast?"

The hawk groaned.

"I mean," said Billina, "good manners would

have dictated waiting for an invitation, or at least asking leave."

The hawk groaned.

"That was quite a crash and quite a fall," she said. She lifted up one foot, put it down, then lifted up the other foot and put it down.

"Perhaps this is no time for me to stand on ceremony. Are you all right?"

The hawk groaned.

Billina bent over him and was so intent on studying his injuries that she did not see Dorothy scamper out of the yard.

Billina's maternal instincts took over. She marched into her coop and flapped out again carrying a first aid kit in her beak. Clucking and cooing as she worked, she applied iodine to the hawk's cuts and scratches. Then, with deft precision, she bandaged his wrenched wing with a splint made from tongue depressors and gauze. Throughout the whole operation, the hawk said nothing and he tried not to groan, even when the iodine hurt.

"Permit me to introduce myself. I am Thunder Wing and I thank you. Your healing arts are indeed wonderful, Mother Billina," Thunder Wing said when she was done.

A Warning Ignored

"You know who I am?" said Billina, puffing out her feathers with pride.

"Every bird both great and small knows of Billina, the Royal Hen of Oz. The hatching announcements for Dorothy and Daniel went out to everyone," said Thunder Wing. "I, however, have never before heard that you were an excellent nurse as well as a fine bird."

Billina cooed.

"Your ministrations and a few days' rest are sure to render me air-worthy," he continued, "I only hope the fair skies of Oz will be safe when I am well again."

"Whatever do you mean?" asked Billina, bobbing her head and pacing back and forth.

"Yesterday afternoon," Thunder Wing said, "I was sleeping peacefully in my own nest in a forest near the border of Oz when I awoke to a nasty shock. My body had been taken over by a mysterious stranger calling himself Shady, Avenger of the Nome King..." The hawk went on and told Billina the whole story of his flight to the Emerald City.

"That's all very interesting, Thunder Wing," Billina said skeptically, "but whatever became of this Shady character?"

A Warning Ignored

"No doubt he has gone off to work his mischief on some other poor, unsuspecting soul," said Thunder Wing.

"Either that or you had a nightmare," said Billina.

"This was no dream!" cried the hawk.

"Think how it must sound to me since this Shady is nowhere to be seen," said the hen.

"You must believe me," pleaded Thunder Wing. "Princess Ozma and the people of the Emerald City are in great danger!"

"If they are," replied Billina, using her most calming, motherly voice, "there are those who can help better than you can. Regardless as to whether your story is true or not, you've had quite a night. You need rest and food..."

"Billina," said Thunder Wing as a dark thought crossed his mind.

"Yes?" cheeped the hen.

"What if Shady has kidnapped one of your little chicks?"

"We'll just see about that!" said Billina. "Dorothy?" she called.

"Yes, mother?" peeped a chorus of little voices.

"Daniel?" she called.

"Yes, mother?" peeped another chorus of little

voices.

"Everyone's accounted for," she said. "Now, as I was saying, you need rest and food. Stay here, in the shelter of the yard. All I have is corn. Not your usual fare, I suppose. I hope it will do."

"If it is good enough for the Royal Hen of Oz, it is good enough for me," said Thunder Wing.

Billina collected him a pile of kernels and he set to work eating them. The hawk sighed. He tried to be content with corn, to ignore the throbbing in his wing and to still the worry in his heart.

The Incident in the Palace Laundry

"Where are we going?" peeped Dorothy as Shady propelled her into the cellar of Princess Ozma's palace.

"Just you wait and see," said Shady. He was looking for the best route down while remaining out of sight.

"I love a mystery!" said Dorothy. "Shall I try to guess?"

"Shush," said Shady.

Shady and the little chick entered a labyrinth of corridors, dimly lit by yellow, glowing globes hanging from the vaulted ceilings. Servants bustled up and down, back and forth, going about the business of running Princess Ozma's palace.

"I don't have permission to be down here," said Dorothy. "I'm going to get in trouble."

A passing servant heard the little chick's peeping. Quick as a wink, Shady pulled them into the shadows and the servant did not stay to investigate.

"Oooo!" said Dorothy. "You got me out of

trouble that time! You must be my best friend!"

"That's right," said Shady, "you are allowed to be down here because you are with me, but we are on a *secret* mission, so we must not be seen or heard by anyone."

"I'll be quiet," said Dorothy.

"Good," said Shady. He could tell the little chick trusted him and he planned to take advantage of that.

The little chick, firmly controlled by Shady, started down the corridor again.

"What kind of secret mission are we on?" piped Dorothy before they had gone five feet.

"We're at War," said Shady. "Now, remember what I said about being quiet!"

"WAR!" cried Dorothy, unable to contain herself.

Shady tried to shush her to silence.

"I've never played War before!" said Dorothy in a loud, stagy whisper.

More passing servants heard the little chick's peeping (and Shady's shushing, as well). It took some fast moves for Shady to keep them out of sight.

"You must be quiet," Shady said. "Princess Ozma has reason to believe that enemies have invaded her palace. If you aren't quiet, we will be discovered before we can stop them."

"That's exciting!" said Dorothy. "I've never been on a secret mission before, but I already love them!"

As they talked, they came to the entrance to the Palace Laundry and Shady saw this as an excellent place for his first piece of mischief.

"Come with me," said Shady. He fluttered Dorothy's wings, carrying them into the Palace Laundry.

The Palace Laundry was a mechanical wonderland, designed and built by master craftsmen, Smith & Tinker. Rank upon rank of gleaming pipes studded with spigots and faucets carried water from burnished copper heating hoppers covered with dials and gauges to vast, shining washing and rinsing vats. Glass tanks filled with soap hung on swivels controlled by gears and pulleys above the washing vats.

On one side of the Palace Laundry, mechanical hands sorted clothing and linens into neat piles. Conveyor belts carried the clothing and linens to the washing vats where they were stirred by giant agitators. More conveyor belts carried the clean clothes and linens to the rinsing vats where they soaked, then ran through a creaking ringer. Still more conveyor belts carried the clothes and linens to drying racks where mechanical hands laid them out. Big fans blew air across the drying clothes and more mechanical hands plucked them from the racks, placed them on pressing boards, pressed them flat and folded them neatly, leaving them in stacks on the other side of the Palace Laundry. The fresh, clean smell of warm water and soap and the sound of gurgling, churgling, chuffing and clanking filled the air.

The Palace Washer Woman, mistress of this marvelous mass of machinery, moved among the hoppers and vats, fans and racks, pressers and folders, eyeing the quality of work and keeping the machines calibrated. She was a tall, broad-shouldered woman with big hands and was wearing a spotless white smock over her powder blue dress. Her long hair was neatly pinned in a bun on her head. Although it was almost impossible to hear over the noise of the Laundry, she was singing at the top of her lungs.

"What is all this?" peeped Dorothy in awe.

"That," said Shady as they flew over the head of the Palace Washer Woman, "is a wicked witch. As I suspected, she is in here making a witch's brew with all this equipment. She plans on casting a dastardly spell on the palace!"

Together, Shady and Dorothy flew up to the ceiling.

"She can't be a wicked witch," said Dorothy. "She's wearing white!"

"That's her disguise," said Shady. "All of this is disguised. How else do you think she was able to sneak into Princess Ozma's palace?"

"Oooo!" said the little chick, "I never thought of that!"

"That's what you have me for," said Shady.

"It's our secret mission to stop her, right?" said the little chick.

"Precisely!" said Shady. He was overjoyed with how well things were going.

"What do we have to do?" asked Dorothy.

"I'll show you," said Shady.

He pushed the little chick harder than he had as yet and sent her zooming up and down over the washing vats. Under his prodding, the chick opened spigots so that more hot water poured into the vats. Dorothy set the agitators spinning as fast as they could and dumped all the soap from the glass tanks into the washing vats. Shady had been afraid the little chick would not be strong enough to accomplish all this, but everything was so well oiled it moved at a feather's touch. Dorothy and Shady worked so fast that they were done before the Palace Washer Woman saw what they were up to.

"Hey!" she shrieked, "Stop messing with the cleaning!"

"The wicked witch sees us!" cried Dorothy.

"Don't worry," said Shady soothingly, flying Dorothy up out of the Washer Woman's reach. "We've wrecked her witch's brew. Now all we have to do is stop her from regaining her power."

As Shady spoke, first one, then a second and then a third washing vat overflowed, spilling water and suds onto the floor. The agitators spun wildly, whipping all the soap into a thick, bubbly froth that flowed after the sudsy water.

"I'll be drowned for sure," shrieked the Palace Washer Woman over the groaning, clanking sounds coming from the stressed machinery. She ran up a ladder to a catwalk over the vats to turn off the spigots.

Shady was ready for this and had positioned himself and little Dorothy at the controls for the mechanical hands. Under Shady's guidance, one pair of hands reached up, plucked the poor Washer

The Incident in the Palace Laundry

Woman from her perch and dumped her head first into one of the frothing vats. Great spurts of soap bubbles shot from the vat and the Washer Woman howled in rage.

The Palace Laundry was already several feet deep in water and foam. All the nice, neat piles of fresh, clean clothes and linens had been soaked. The poor, bedraggled Palace Washer Woman was desperately trying to climb out of the vat, blowing soap bubbles out her mouth.

"Mission accomplished!" said Shady as he surveyed the scene. "Let us go find another battle to fight!"

As Shady flew little Dorothy out the door of the Palace Laundry he heard the Palace Washer Woman shouting, "Just wait until your mother hears about this you wretched little chicken!"

The Battle of
the Royal Kitchens

Dorothy, propelled by Shady, rocketed down the hall and around the corner, then flew willy-nilly down that corridor. Once they were well away from the Palace Laundry and out of sight in a shadowy alcove, Shady let them rest.

"What a terrible mess we left behind," panted little Dorothy, preening soap suds from her wings. "Was it enough to stop the wicked witch? After all, her equipment was all still there."

"Don't worry about that," said Shady. "We stopped her spell in time and Princess Ozma's servants will hear her shrieking and come in time to stop her from working any other magical mischief. Now that you've thwarted a wicked witch, what do you think of secret missions?"

"I think I should like to spend the rest of my life as a spy," said Dorothy, shaking her tail feathers dry.

"That can be arranged," said Shady with a chuckle.

"You could do that for me?" asked Dorothy.

"Of course I could," said Shady. "I am the secretest secret agent in all of Oz!"

"You're the best friend I've ever had," said Dorothy, "and we've never even met before! Who are you, anyway?"

"The time is not yet right for me to reveal myself," said Shady. "For now, I must work through you to help save Princess Ozma from the enemies that have so cleverly surrounded her. That wicked witch was only the first. Let's go on to our next secret mission in order to ensure Princess Ozma's safety and comfort."

"What is our next mission?" peeped Dorothy.

Never having been in Princess Ozma's palace before, Shady had only the vaguest idea of what might be in the cellars.

"Just be quiet and come along like a good chick," he said.

Dorothy and Shady moved on through the Palace cellars with Dorothy peeping away about this and that and Shady keeping them out of sight of Princess Ozma's servants. After a few minutes, they came to the Royal Kitchens.

The Royal Kitchens were at least five times the size of the Palace Laundry. While the Palace Laundry had been a study of gleaming, precise machinery working in orderly fashion, the Royal Kitchens were a dizzying swirl of chaotic activity. People ran every which way, calling out to each other as they went. Pots, pans, trays and tins seemed to fly through the air without any rhyme or reason. The Royal Chef was a tremendously tall, rail-thin man with a nose the size of a turnip. He wore a huge, floppy white hat and stood in the midst of the mayhem, shouting orders at the top of his lungs. No one noticed the little chick fluttering above the hustle and bustle.

"Here's where we carry out our next secret mission," said Shady.

"What do we have to do?" asked Dorothy eagerly.

"He," said Shady, pointing at the Royal Chef, "is planning on making Princess Ozma ill. We must stop him."

"How could he ever think of such a thing?" said Dorothy.

"Some people just have a mean streak," said Shady.

"How are we going to stop him?" asked Dorothy.

"Let's take a look around and see what we can do," said Shady.

Under Shady's guidance, Dorothy flew around

the Royal Kitchens in a wide circle. They went past the ovens where breads, pastries and cakes were baking. They circled over pots of soup, bubbling over the fire. They passed racks and crates of apples and pears, plums and peaches, grapes and other exotic fruits. Great stacks of pots and pans and trays stood everywhere, many of them teetering precariously. Everything was bathed in dreamy warmth from the ovens and washed with the heavenly scents of baking and stewing.

At one end of the kitchen stood the most extraordinary culinary creation Shady had ever seen. It was a cake, but to call it merely a cake would be like calling Princess Ozma's Royal Palace a building.

First of all, it measured ten feet long and eight and a half feet wide at its base. It rose to a height of five feet at its corner stacks and to a height of over six feet at its center.

Second of all, it was elaborately decorated. The entire surface of the cake was coated in a soft, gooey marshmallow and whipped cream icing and sprinkled with sugar all the colors of the rainbow. The entire base was dotted with chocolate chips and all five stacks were studded with rising spirals of chocolate, butterscotch and caramel. Bridges made of cinnamon and licorice spanned the canyons between the stacks and flags made of spun sugar flew from the peaks.

"That," said Shady, "is what he plans on using to make Princess Ozma ill!"

"That makes sense," said Dorothy. "It's pretty but it looks like it could give anyone a tummy ache, especially if they ate it all!"

"Get away from my masterpiece you ridiculous little chicken!" bellowed the Royal Chef.

Without any urging from Shady, Dorothy flew straight up into the air, narrowly missing being caught by the Chef.

"He's on to us!" cried Shady.

"Who let that feathered flitterhead in here?" yelled the Royal Chef. He leapt into the air, trying to catch Dorothy. Again, without any urging, Dorothy darted away.

"Catch it! Catch it!" shrieked the Royal Chef.

All the other servants threw their hands in the air and ran around, shouting and yelling.

"Quick," said Shady, "we must create a diversion."

Under Shady's expert guidance, Dorothy flew up near the ceiling. Heads craned. Dorothy zoomed towards a stack of pots and the servants ran towards her. Dorothy knocked the pots over, sending many of the running servants sprawling.

The battle was on!

Pots and pans, knives and ladles, trays and rolling pins all flew through the air. Shady had Dorothy bobbing and weaving, looping and spiralling this way and that. He always positioned her so that each carefully aimed utensil or piece of crockery narrowly missed, but went on to brain another servant or tumble a stack of pans or overturn a cooking pot.

The Royal Chef was beyond words. He stood on a table near the cake waving a cleaver in the air, shrieking. His face was red as a beet and all the blood vessels in his neck were standing out.

Most of the servants were either out cold or had retreated to the sides of the kitchen, afraid to fight any more.

"Now for the final blow," said Shady.

He made Dorothy flutter down towards the Royal Chef.

The Royal Chef roared, waved the cleaver and lunged at Dorothy.

Dorothy wanted to soar away, but Shady held her firmly. As the Royal Chef lunged, Shady

pulled back oh so very slowly, making the Royal Chef lean forward without taking a step. Then the Royal Chef lost his footing altogether and plunged head first into the gooey, marshmallow and whipped cream icing of the gigantic cake. He was coated with the sticky, gelatinous mass. Chocolate chips studded his turnip nose. Multicolored sugar adorned his floppy hat. The servants of the Royal Kitchens who were still standing fought hard to keep from bursting into gales of laughter.

As Shady propelled Dorothy out the window of the Royal Kitchens he heard the Royal Chef shouting, "Just wait until your mother hears about this you wretched little chicken!"

Billina's Dilemma

Billina and Thunder Wing were enjoying the bright, warm sunshine. They had been passing the time chatting about this and that while the Dorothys and the Daniels scampered about peeping happily. The scene was so calm and peaceful that all of the hawk's worries had evaporated.

The morning was turning towards noon and Billina was beginning to wonder what she should serve her guest for lunch when two new visitors arrived.

First came the Palace Washer Woman. Her clothes were dripping, her neat bun had collapsed and her wet hair had coiled up in hundreds of tight little curls. A thin trail of soap bubbles still blew from her smock. They darted and spun behind her as she walked.

Right behind her came the Royal Chef. His hat was jammed down over one eye and was still coated with marshmallow and whipped cream. A light dusting of multicolored sugar covered his apron and several dollops of chocolate chips clung to his pants.

"What have we here?" said Billina as she rose

to greet her visitors.

"Royal Hen of Oz!" said the Palace Washer Woman.

"Mother of all Chickens!" shouted the Royal Chef.

The Palace Washer Woman turned on the Royal Chef.

"Wait your turn!" she said hotly. "I was here first. What's become of manners in these dark, declining days?"

"I'm here on urgent business," retorted the Royal Chef. "What can a hen care about dirty clothes?"

"No call to go insulting me!" said the Palace Washer Woman. "After all, what can a hen care about sugar and spice?" She turned her back on the Royal Chef, blocking him off from Billina.

"Royal Hen of Oz," she went on as the Royal Chef bounced up and down behind her, "your little hatchling, Dorothy, has just created a ruckus in my laundry — and it's a ruckus like no such ruckus as I've ever had to contend with in all my days. It'll be hours before I get the place mopped up, a day before I get my machines reset and three before I get the clothes and the linens resorted, recleaned, redried, repressed and back to their rightful owners — if I can ever figure out whose is whose!"

"Mother of all chickens," bellowed the Royal Chef, stepping around from behind the dripping Palace Washer Woman, "your little cherub has set my servants throwing pots and pans all over creation and has forced me to utterly destroy, demolish and desecrate the finest creation of my long, delicious career. Now Ozma will have to make do with second rate food prepared without the proper care."

"My laundry a shambles. My work ruined!" wailed the Palace Washer Woman.

"My kitchens a shambles. My masterpiece ruined!" shouted the Royal Chef.

"Disaster and filth!" shrieked the Palace Washer Woman.

"Calamity and famine!" hollered the Royal Chef.

"Unending grief and torment!" wailed the Palace Washer Woman.

"The ruin of all hope and death at an early age!" wept the Royal Chef.

Each shouted louder and louder, trying to drown out the lament of the other.

"This is the end of cooking and cleaning as we know it, and it's all because of your little chicken!"

they shrieked together.

For her part, Billina preened her feathers and let her two visitors run out of breath.

"I really don't know what to say," she began when the noise died down. "Dorothy's never acted this way before. She used to be such a good egg. I don't know what could have gotten into her."

"She needs discipline!" said the Royal Chef.

"A firm, motherly hand," said the Palace Washer Woman.

Then, they began shouting all over again. Billina looked at them long and hard, shifting from one foot to the other and flicking her tail feathers in irritation.

"Billina," said Thunder Wing. His strong, gentle voice cut through the tumult from the two irate visitors.

"You are going to tell me that what you feared has actually happened, aren't you?" said Billina.

"That is correct," said the hawk. "I am afraid I have brought tragedy and a bad reputation to your family by transporting Shady here to your very yard."

"Don't worry yourself about that," said Billina. "I never would have given much credit to your story, but I forget that queer things have a way of

Billina's Dilemma

happening in Oz. If Shady is at the bottom of all this, he would have found me no matter what you did. The Nome King and I have had our differences in the past and they have nothing to do with you. The question now is what am I going to do?"

"I'll say that's the question!" shouted both the Palace Washer Woman and the Royal Chef.

"Of course it's the question," the Palace Washer Woman snapped at the Royal Chef.

"Didn't you hear what I said or were you too busy listening to yourself," bellowed the Royal Chef. "I said, the question now is what are you going to do?"

"The question isn't what I'm going to do," said the Palace Washer Woman. "The question is what is *she* going to do?"

Billina ignored the two shouting people.

"You told me that this Shady was an apparition that attacked your shadow and then made you do things you didn't want to do," she said to the hawk.

"That is true," said Thunder Wing.

"How on earth could anyone do something like that?"

"I do not know," he said. "My shadow did not

understand it either."

"We're facing the end of life in the Royal Palace as we know it and the only hen who can save us won't even lift a feather!" the Palace Washer Woman and the Royal Chef both sobbed. For consolation, they threw their arms around each other.

"Well, however Shady did this, it is a scientific marvel, if nothing else," said Billina. "Therefore, I must consult with the sharpest mind in the Emerald City to see if he can help me come up with a solution before Shady forces my daughter to do any more wicked deeds."

"Do you think the Scarecrow can help at a time like this?" said Thunder Wing.

"Although my dear friend the Scarecrow is wise," said Billina, "I need help from one who is thoroughly educated in scientific matters."

"You're going to pay a visit to H.M. Wogglebug, T.E.?" asked Thunder Wing in awe.

"He's the only one who can help, if he'll stoop to talking with one as unschooled as I," said Billina.

With that the Royal Hen of Oz set off for the College of Art and Athletic Perfection to find the Wogglebug, leaving Thunder Wing behind to watch over the Dorothys and the Daniels.

Meanwhile, the Palace Washer Woman and the Royal Chef had discovered they liked hugging each other very much. They had forgotten all about their troubles and did not even notice Billina's departure. They remained in Billina's yard for some time.

Nick and Jack Under Attack

After flying out the window of the Royal Kitchens, Shady took Dorothy up to a balcony overlooking a goldfish pond in the Palace Gardens. There, the little bird and Shady rested under a potted lemon tree. A breeze smelling of marigolds and lilacs cooled them. The sound of rustling leaves soothed them.

Shady was confident that he had caused as much trouble as he could in the palace cellars, at least for the time being. If he tried any more tricks, he was sure they would be caught. Now, he wanted to take a few minutes to rest, and then see what mischief he could cause in the upper floors of the palace.

In spite of this lovely, peaceful setting Dorothy was tired of being a secret agent. Her wings ached. She missed her mother, her brothers and sisters. She tried to get up and start flying back to her yard, but Shady held her in place.

"Where are you racing off to, little one?" he asked.

"I want to go home," said Dorothy.

75

"Aren't you having fun?" asked Shady.

"Not anymore," said Dorothy.

"I thought you liked secret missions," said Shady.

"I do," replied Dorothy. "But I've been on two already. Couldn't we go home? We could rest and eat some sweet, juicy corn and tell the Daniels all about how we saved Princess Ozma. We could go on more secret missions tomorrow." She tried to start flying again, but Shady held her firmly in place.

"Let me go!" Dorothy peeped.

"Tsk, tsk, tsk," said Shady. "I must say that I'm disappointed in you. I had hoped you were more mature than this. I selected you to be a secret agent because I thought you'd be willing to sacrifice a little to help defend Princess Ozma from her enemies. You said I was your best friend, and I had hoped that you were mine, too. I see I was mistaken."

"Please don't be upset with me," said Dorothy.

"What else should I be?" asked Shady with a sigh.

Little Dorothy felt terrible. Shady had her right where he wanted her.

"What do you want me to do?" asked Dorothy.

Nick and Jack Under Attack

"Let's sit here and enjoy the breeze for a little while," said Shady. "Ozma's enemies will reveal themselves in due time and we will know what to do on our next secret mission."

"OK," said Dorothy. "That sounds fine to me."

They continued to sit on the balcony enjoying the breezes. After a few minutes, they heard voices coming from the balcony above them.

"We should go investigate," said Shady, hoping this would give him a new chance for making trouble.

Although Dorothy was still tired, she did not want to disappoint her new friend. She did not complain as Shady urged her into the air.

Shady was overcome with glee as soon as he and Dorothy cleared the railing of the upper balcony.

Two of the most famous, beloved personages in all of Oz stood on the balcony chatting with each other.

The first person was dressed in a bright red shirt, a pink vest with white polka-dots and baggy purple trousers. His head was a shiny orange pumpkin carved with a smiling, jagged-toothed face. Knobby stick hands stuck out far from his sleeves, his long stick legs stretched out from his pants before entering his well-worn shoes. This person was none other than Princess Ozma's oldest friend, Jack Pumpkinhead.

The second person was made entirely of brightly polished, nickel-plated tin. His hat was a gleaming funnel and his face was cleverly sculpted metal. Neat rows of rivets attached his arms and legs to his body and held the plates for his chest, shoulders and back in place. In one hand he held a mighty axe with a long, gracefully curved oak handle. The sunlight sparkled and shown on his polished surface. This person was none other than Nick Chopper, the Tin Woodman, Emperor of the Winkies and trusted advisor and fast friend of Princess Ozma.

"What a perfect chance for more wickedness!" Shady thought as they fluttered in the air, a few inches from the edge of the balcony. But he had forgotten to reckon with little Dorothy.

"Mr. Pumpkinhead! Mr. Chopper!" peeped the little chick. Like Shady, she was also overjoyed to see these two famous friends of Ozma, but for very different reasons. She was sure that her mysterious friend would want to enlist their help in fighting the princess's enemies.

"Why look!" cried the Tin Woodman with

delight. "I do believe that it's little Dorothy."

Jack looked down, hoping to see Dorothy Gale of Kansas, but there was nobody there.

As soon as Dorothy had peeped out her greeting, Shady forced her down below the level of the balcony.

"Your heart seems to have run ahead of your head, my brilliant friend," said Jack. "I don't see Dorothy anywhere."

"She just dipped down below the balcony," said Nick Chopper. "I think she's playing a game with us!"

"How can Dorothy dip down below the balcony?" asked the Pumpkinhead.

"Is your pumpkin beginning to spoil?" said the Tin Woodman. "All a little chick has to do is flutter her wings and she can rise or dip anywhere."

"Oh!" cried Jack, clapping his hands to his head. "You mean little Dorothy from Billina, not little Dorothy from Kansas!"

Meanwhile, below the balcony, Dorothy was puzzled.

"Why did you make me hide from our friends?" she asked.

"Caution is the order of the day," said Shady.

"We must investigate closely to make sure that these two are who they seem to be."

"Don't be silly," said Dorothy. "That's Jack Pumpkinhead and Nick Chopper. Everyone knows who they are."

"The wicked witch and the mad poisoner weren't who they seemed to be, were they?" asked Shady.

A terrible, unhappy thought was forming in Dorothy's little mind. "Maybe they really were what they seemed. Maybe you tricked me into thinking they were Ozma's enemies just like you are trying to make me suspicious of Mr. Pumpkinhead and Mr. Chopper. Maybe *you're* the one I should be suspicious of."

Two faces appeared over the edge of the balcony.

"Look," said the Tin Woodman. "It is little Dorothy!"

"Hello chick," called Jack, waving. "Why don't you come to visit?"

"Help me!" cried Dorothy. "I'm a prisoner and being forced to make mischief against my will!"

"Hush," Shady hissed to the chick. Then, to throw the Tin Woodman and Jack Pumpkinhead off the track he made his voice sound like

Dorothy's and said, "Ha, ha! Did I fool you?"

"I don't understand what's going on here!" said Jack. "Little Dorothy has two voices and there's only one of her!"

"It breaks my heart to see her so scared," said the Tin Woodman.

"Whatever you do, don't start crying now," said Jack. "I don't know where your oil can is."

"Help me!" peeped Dorothy. "Won't you please help me!"

"Ha, ha, ha!" chimed in Shady. "Isn't this a great joke." To Dorothy he hissed, "Shut up! You're going to ruin everything!"

"You've already ruined enough, yourself!" retorted Dorothy.

"I still can't see where that other voice is coming from," murmured Jack. He leaned out from the balcony as far as he could.

Shady flew Dorothy up towards the Pumpkinhead.

"Catch hold of me!" Shady cried, imitating Dorothy's voice.

"Be careful, Mr. Pumpkinhead!" cried Dorothy.

Shady kept Dorothy just out of Jack's reach. The Pumpkinhead leaned out too far.

"I've almost got yooooouuuuu..."

The Nome King's Shadow in Oz

"Look out!" hollered the Tin Woodman.

But it was too late! Jack's beautiful orange pumpkinhead slipped off his neck and spun down, down, down. He desperately stretched out his long, spindly arms in a futile attempt to catch his head. But he lost his balance and his lanky body tumbled spike over heels off the balcony. With a tremendous splash, his big round head landed in the goldfish pond below. A second splash announced the arrival of his body. Jack's arms waved wildly searching for his missing head as the floating pumpkin shouted directions.

"How could you do that?" cried Dorothy.

Shady could no longer contain himself.

"I am the mighty Shady, Avenger of the Nome King! See how the friends of Princess Ozma fall before me! Now, Tin Woodman, prepare to meet your doom!"

"A little to the left! Or do I mean right?" shouted Jack's pumpkin from below.

"Stop it!" shrieked the little chick.

Shady made Dorothy swoop towards the Tin Woodman, planning to leap from Dorothy to Nick Chopper and take him over. But Shady did not take Nick's shiny body into account. Just as Shady began stretching out for the Tin Woodman,

Nick and Jack Under Attack

the sun bounced off the highly polished metal and scorched him.

"Yiee!" cried Shady, pulling back and making Dorothy soar up out of the way.

"Help me! Help me!" peeped the little chick.

The Tin Woodman grabbed for the chick and again the sunlight bounced off him and burned Shady.

Smarting in pain, Shady forced Dorothy to make a hasty retreat.

"I'll be back!" Shady bellowed as they flew away.

"Have courage, little friend!" cried the Tin Woodman. "As soon as I put my friend back together we will find you and save you from this fiend!" Then, the Tin Woodman ran to help Jack Pumpkinhead.

"Now," Shady said to Dorothy, "You will do exactly as I say or you will never see your family again. Do you understand?"

"Yes," said Dorothy, quaking in fear.

"Good," said Shady. "Now I am taking you to Princess Ozma's throne room where we will carry out our final mission!"

Laughing wickedly, Shady flew the shivering Dorothy back into Princess Ozma's Palace.

Billina Asks the Wogglebug

The Emerald City campus of the Royal College of Art and Athletic Perfection stood on the other side of the central square from Princess Ozma's Palace. The College was a large, ivy-covered brick building studded with windows whose wooden frames were painted white.

Billina flew through the front doors and came to a landing on the marble floor of the College lobby. Long halls lined with doors stretched away on either side of the lobby. A wide, curving staircase of marble, with ornate wooden banisters swept up to the floors above.

The whole College was sunk in a studious, whispery hush, but this did not slow Billina down one bit. She strutted down the hall to a door marked "DEAN'S OFFICE" and marched in.

Inside, an oversized, brightly colored butterfly sat behind a desk shuffling papers. Behind the butterfly stood the door to an inner office marked "H.M. WOGGLEBUG, T.E. - DEAN."

"Do you have an appointment?" asked the butterfly.

"No," said Billina, starting towards the door to the Wogglebug's office, "but this is an emergency."

"Are you enrolled in the College?" asked the butterfly, blocking the door with her wings.

"No," said Billina, "but I need Professor Wogglebug's help."

"The Dean is very busy and is not to be disturbed," said the butterfly.

Billina took a step back and launched herself at the butterfly. The butterfly let out a shrill shriek and fell to the floor. Billina was reaching for the door when H.M. Wogglebug, T.E., pulled it open from inside. His glasses were on crooked. His antennae were askew. He looked for all the world as if he had just woken up.

"How dare you disturb my meditations?" snapped the Wogglebug.

"I'm terribly sorry," said Billina, "but I have come to you with a most pressing problem that concerns the safety of Princess Ozma herself. It is only with your superior intellect and extraordinary learning that I can hope to find a solution to this problem."

"Is that so?" said the Wogglebug, beaming. "In that case, step into my office and we shall see what I can do for you."

Billina Asks the Wogglebug

With a flutter of her tail feathers at the gaudy butterfly, Billina marched into the Wogglebug's office.

H.M. Wogglebug, T.E. sat at his desk eyeing the Royal Hen of Oz. The Wogglebug's office was a jumbled combination library and scientific laboratory. Books and equipment were scattered everywhere.

"What terrible calamity brings you flapping to my door?" asked the Wogglebug.

Billina clucked out the whole story Thunder Wing had told her about Shady, Avenger of the Nome King, then went on to tell about her missing chick and the complaints from the Palace Washer Woman and the Royal Chef. As she spoke, she strutted up and down. Her head bobbed from side to side. The Wogglebug listened to it all with an unbelieving expression on his face.

"Even now," said Billina, "I am sure that my daughter is being forced to perform even worse mischief. No one in the Emerald City is safe. What are we to do?"

"Don't be so quick to cry, 'The sky is falling!'" said the Wogglebug.

"This could be a matter of life and death!" crowed Billina.

"Given that you and a hawk are two of the prime witnesses and your chick is the prime perpetrator," said the Wogglebug, "I'm inclined to believe that there is a feather weight matter and a bird-brained affair from start to finish."

"You really bug me when you talk like that," said Billina.

"Do you honestly believe that the Nome King has hatched some nefarious plot to feather his nest by somehow mysteriously making your daughter misbehave?" said the Wogglebug.

"It is more than possible," said Billina. "Since I was responsible for his defeat when he tried to hold Princess Ozma prisoner, the Nome King has good reason to want to catch me in his web while trying to sting Princess Ozma."

"That would indeed be a foul plot," said the Wogglebug, "but I have a hard time believing something that lurks in the shadows could ever come home to roost with such power."

"The fate of the Emerald City hangs on a thread and my family is at stake," said Billina. "Your bemused attitude and constant puns are really starting to tick me off. Are you going to help me solve this mystery or not?"

"I would be happy to talk turkey," said the

Billina Asks the Wogglebug

Wogglebug, "but your problem sounds so implausible, I think you need a bantam weight intellect rather than my own waspish wit and heavy weight mind to believe it, much less solve it."

Billina cleared her throat slowly. "I will not stoop to your level. I am too high on the pecking order for that," she said with great dignity. "The bearers of bad news are rarely understood before it is too late. Very well. Time is wasting and the peril is mounting. If you won't be any help, I'll find a solution myself!"

Billina paced up and down while the Wogglebug sat behind his desk and smirked.

"Let me see," she said, "if the Avenger of the Nome King works through people's shadows then he must somehow be a shadow himself. Therefore, I'm trying to catch a shadow. Since opposites attract, I'll need something that is the opposite of a shadow. Shadows are dark. The opposite of dark is light, so I'll need light. But that won't be enough. The Avenger of the Nome King is also crooked, so I'll need crooked light to catch him. What can I use to bend light? Of course! A mirror."

Billina flapped up onto the Wogglebug's

Billina Asks the Wogglebug

laboratory table where she found a hand mirror and a small lantern that were sitting there.

"Are you going to give your daughter a chance to reflect on her wrongs?" asked the Wogglebug.

"First," said Billina in a haughty tone, "I am going to save my daughter and rid the Emerald City of this peril. Then, I am going to tell Princess Ozma about your scandalous conduct, and when I do she will certainly be as mad as a hornet. I am sure you will feel like an ant when she is done with you."

So saying, Billina grasped the mirror and lantern. In order to save time, she flew through the window of the Wogglebug's office.

"Whatever is afoot," said the Wogglebug, "I have to see it." He started after Billina, but he exited through the door.

The Princess in Peril

Princess Ozma, dainty and beloved girl ruler of
Oz, sat in her Council Chambers, meeting with
her dear friends and devoted servants, the
Cowardly Lion and the Hungry Tiger.

Princess Ozma had a beautiful, heart-shaped
face with an elegant jawline, pert nose and rosy
red lips. Her open, caring face was framed with
thick tresses of wavy black hair which fell in a
cascade down her back. These silky locks were
held in place with a delicately crafted silver
headband. The headband was decorated with an
emblem in which the letters "O-Z" entwined with
each other in a circle. This emblem rested in the
center of Ozma's forehead.

The Princess of Oz wore a filmy gown woven of
purple, blue, red, yellow and green which
represented each of the major regions of Oz. The
gown's colors shifted prismatically every time
Ozma moved.

Ozma's Council Chamber was a large room with
elaborate parquet wood floors and an arching,
marble ceiling. High windows overlooking the

fountains and mazes of the Royal Gardens lined
one wall. A long oak table with comfortable,
padded oak chairs stood at one end of the Council
Chamber.

At this time of day, the sun was at such a point
in the sky that its rays only came in the window
nearest the table. The rest of the Council
Chamber was sunk in cool, dim shade. As the
afternoon progressed and the sun moved across
the sky, its rays would shine through more and
more of the windows until the whole chamber was
warm and bright.

Princess Ozma sat in one of the chairs at the
head of the table. The Cowardly Lion and Hungry
Tiger, being too large for the chairs and having no
need for them either, sat on their haunches on
either side of the Princess. They were just
wrapping up their business.

"Once again," said Ozma, "you have done an
excellent job. I thank you!" She leaned forward
and planted a kiss first on the furry cheek of the
Cowardly Lion and then on the equally furry
cheek of the Hungry Tiger.

Both cats blushed beneath their coats.

"I must say," Ozma continued, "that I am
surprised to see you so soon. I did not expect you

to return for three more days."

The Cowardly Lion cleared his throat and said, "There is one more thing we must discuss, Your Highness."

He then told Ozma the whole story of how a shadow calling himself Shady, Avenger of the Nome King, had attacked him in the forests near the border of Oz.

"If anyone else told me such an outlandish tale," said Ozma, "I would think they were imagining things or trying to play a joke on me. But since you are the messenger, I must take this very seriously."

"Then," said the Cowardly Lion, "I am glad that I am the one to tell you even though the news is so frightening!"

"I am curious to see what mischief the Nome King thinks he can get away with here where I am surrounded by such good and faithful friends," said Ozma.

As Ozma was speaking, little Dorothy, still in Shady's thrall, came bobbing through the door.

"Hello, little one," said Ozma. "It is a pleasure to see you."

Ozma was never too busy with affairs of state to enjoy a visit from even her smallest subjects.

The Princess in Peril

The little chick was so terrified she peeped, "Hello Princess Ozma. I am very glad to see you today," even though she was yearning to cry out a warning.

At Shady's urging, Dorothy fluttered up and started to fly towards Ozma. She was so tired she could barely lift her wings.

Ozma thought she heard a wicked laugh coming from the little chick, but she was not sure. Shady's laugh, for that is what it was, was drowned out by two other sudden, surprising noises.

First, the Cowardly Lion let out a tremendous, ear shattering roar. Second, even before the echoes died down from the Cowardly Lion's roar, Billina flew through the window of the Council Chamber with a wild flapping of her wings and much urgent squawking. She was carrying the lantern and the mirror.

"Your highness!" cried the Cowardly Lion, "Beware! My shadow has just told me that this chick carries your mortal enemy!"

"Dorothy!" cried Billina, "what shameful mischief are you planning now?"

"Mama!" peeped the little chick, "Save me!"

Ozma, who had jumped to her feet in surprise,

said, "Who comes into the heart of my realm and threatens my subjects?"

Shady laughed again and, making Dorothy hover in mid-air, shrieked, "I am the Mighty Shady, Avenger of the Nome King. I have come to bring you to your knees and to make all Oz tremble in fear for having wronged the Nome King's honor!"

"My shadow has fought this fiend before and now we will fight him again," roared the Cowardly Lion. He leapt straight over the oak table at little Dorothy.

Shady propelled the little chick, who was peeping with fright, out of the Cowardly Lion's way.

"If you are going to take up eating babies," called the Hungry Tiger, "at least you could pick one who was a little juicier."

"Don't hurt my daughter!" squawked Billina.

Shady laughed wickedly. "You'll have to hurt the little one in order to stop me. She is my prisoner and must do everything I command!" he shouted.

The Cowardly Lion growled. His tail whipped from side to side.

"We cannot attack my daughter," Billina called

to the Cowardly Lion. "We must attack her shadow."

"I am not little Dorothy's shadow," cried Shady, "I am Shady, Avenger of the Nome King, who has come all the way from the land of the Nomes to bring you to ruin!"

The Cowardly Lion poised to spring again.

"That's not the way!" called Billina. "The only way to catch a shadow is with light!"

The Cowardly Lion did not spring, but he still held himself tense and watchful.

Shady was frightened by these words. "You'll never stop me!" he shouted, hoping to scare Billina off.

Billina was not so easily thwarted. Keeping a wary eye on Shady and Dorothy, she touched down for a moment and lit the lantern. Then, she launched herself into the air again and flew in circles around and around Shady and Dorothy.

At that moment, H.M. Wogglebug, T.E. arrived. He was stunned to see so many important personages filling Princess Ozma's Council Chamber and to see so much action. To his credit, he remained quiet and observed from a distance.

Billina's lantern poured out brilliant, golden light. Shady made Dorothy bob and weave in an effort to avoid the burning rays of light, but the little chick was so tired she could not move as quickly as Shady tried to make her. Also, Billina's constant circling around and around meant Shady had to keep circling in order to stay safe.

"Catch can't you me, I'm Avengy the Nadir of the Shome King!" Shady cried. He was starting to get very dizzy.

"We almost have him!" Billina called to the stunned bystanders. "Now watch very closely!" She grasped the mirror in her other foot and, as she circled in one direction, she twisted the mirror around and around, bouncing the bright rays off it in a circle moving in the opposite direction.

This clever move took Shady completely by surprise. He was circling around Dorothy to stay out of the way of the lantern's rays and ran headlong into the reflected rays from the mirror. He screamed in pain as he ran into the light. Everyone in the Council Chamber gasped in shock. The shadow they saw trapped between the two different rays of light had spiky hair standing straight up from its long thin head and a big, roly-poly belly.

"It's a Nome!" everyone gasped.

Shady was gone from sight almost as soon as he

appeared. He curled up underneath Dorothy and made her drop to the floor. Billina came in for a landing and set down the lantern and mirror. She advanced on Shady and her precious little chick from one side. The Cowardly Lion advanced from the other.

"Mama!" wailed Dorothy.

"Let my child go!" cried Billina.

"My shadow and I have got him covered!" growled the Cowardly Lion.

"Curses!" howled Shady, "What has become of my beautiful wickedness?"

But things weren't over quite yet.

"Princess Ozma!" shouted the Tin Woodman, who was dripping wet and creaking loudly, as he burst into the Council Chamber.

"You are in great danger!" shouted Jack Pumpkinhead, coming in behind him with his head askew and his clothes dripping.

Billina and the Cowardly Lion dropped their guard in surprise and Shady seized the moment. With a cry of triumph, he unhooked his shadow hooks from Dorothy and made a break for the door.

Fortunately, H.M. Wogglebug, T.E. and the Hungry Tiger kept their wits about them. The sun had traveled across the sky far enough for it to shine in two more of the Council Chamber's windows. The Wogglebug grabbed the Tin Woodman, and pushed him into the light. Then, using the Tin Woodman's highly polished body just as Billina had used the mirror, the Wogglebug chased Shady into a corner.

The Hungry Tiger instantly understood what the Wogglebug was doing and he leapt into action. Snarling and baring his teeth, he cornered Shady. This gave Billina and the Cowardly Lion a chance to regain their wits. Billina picked up the lantern and the Cowardly Lion stalked forward. Together, they held Shady at bay.

"Billina of Oz," said the Wogglebug, "I will never ridicule another's postulates without first examining their empirical results. Although your reasoning was a bit odd, your method of attack is most effective!"

"Your help is most welcome," said Billina. "I forgive your earlier skeptical comments."

"I say," said the Tin Woodman, "this is certainly a shining example of public service!"

All the while little Dorothy was peeping, "Mama! Mama!" and Shady was wailing, "Don't hurt me! Please don't hurt me!"

The Nome King's Shadow in Oz

Princess Ozma strode forward and raised her hand. "Enough!" she said in a stern voice.

"Please don't hurt me!" Shady wailed.

"Silence!" she said. "Your reign of terror is over, Avenger of the Nome King. Do you surrender?"

"Yes!" cried Shady. "Just get them to take that light off of me!"

"Billina, turn off your lantern. Wogglebug, let go of the Tin Woodman, but friends Lion and Tiger, do not relax your guard until we know we can trust this shadowy form."

Billina and the Wogglebug obeyed Ozma's orders. Billina stepped back and little Dorothy stumbled to her, peeping weakly. Billina folded a protective wing over the little chick.

"Are you quite done?" Ozma asked Shady.

"Oh, yes!" said Shady. "I'll never do this again." He fell on his knees, begging. "Please don't hurt me with those bright lights anymore!"

The Cowardly Lion and the Hungry Tiger growled.

"Do you swear?" asked Ozma.

"Oh, yes!" said Shady.

"Very well," said Ozma, "We will hold you as our prisoner until I have taken stock of all the mischief and damage you have caused."

"Please," begged Shady. "I want to live! Be merciful with me."

"We shall see," said Ozma.

At Princess Ozma's command, carpenters came to the Council Chamber and built a sturdy shadow box to hold Shady.

Shady was so eager to show how cooperative he could be, he jumped into the box as soon as it was finished. He was so glad to be back in the safety of darkness, he did not protest when the lid was nailed on.

"Now," said Ozma, "we have had quite a busy time of it. All of you should go relax. I will issue a decree that everyone who has been involved in these dark doings is invited to dinner in my banquet hall at six o'clock this evening. We will assess the damage Shady has done over dinner and then I will pass judgement."

In The Court of
Princess Ozma of Oz

The group in Princess Ozma's Council Chamber broke up slowly, leaving Shady behind in his prison.

The Cowardly Lion and the Hungry Tiger went for a stroll in the Palace Gardens. H.M. Wogglebug, T.E. took the Tin Woodman back to his laboratory for a thorough polishing and oiling. Jack Pumpkinhead went to a sunny patch on the lawn and spread himself out to dry. Billina carried little Dorothy back home.

Thunder Wing sat in the sun as the Dorothys and the Daniels swarmed over him, peeping with delight. The hawk cooed and laughed with delight as well.

Little Dorothy peered out from under Billina's wing.

"Where have you been?" cried her brothers and sisters.

"I was chick-napped by Shady, Avenger of the Nome King!" said Dorothy.

"No!" cried the other chicks.

"Yes!" said Dorothy. She scampered off to tell them all about it.

"Is the little one all right?" asked Thunder Wing.

"So it seems," said Billina as she watched her chicks run about the grounds outside their coop.

The Palace Washer Woman and the Royal Chef were still there as well. They were holding hands, watching the water splash in the fountain.

"Have you disciplined the young scamp?" the Royal Chef asked in a dreamy voice.

"Yes," said Billina. "Now, I think it's time you went back to work. Princess Ozma has invited everyone who was effected by today's events to a special dinner."

"Oh sweet heavens above!" wailed the Royal Chef. "My kitchen is in ruins and I've no time to plan anything at all!"

"Never fear, my dear," said the Palace Washer Woman. "I have a special stew s-t-r-e-t-c-h-i-n-g recipe I got from my mother for when unexpected company drops in. It takes no time to prepare and goes miles and miles with hungry appetites."

"Isn't she wonderful?" the Royal Chef asked Billina and Thunder Wing. To the Palace Washer Woman he said, "If you put my kitchen help to work on that, I'll see if I can rescue the linens for a proper table service from the ruins of your laundry."

"Isn't he wonderful?" the Palace Washer Woman sighed to the hen and hawk. Then, the pair raced off to prepare for Ozma's dinner.

And what a delectable, delightful feast it was, even though it was overshadowed by what they had to discuss.

Princess Ozma sat at the head of the table. The Cowardly Lion and the Hungry Tiger sat on either side of her, one at her right hand, the other at her left hand. Jack Pumpkinhead and the Tin Woodman sat across from each other, one place down from the great cats. And one place down from these charming people, Billina and the Wogglebug sat opposite each other. The Palace Washer Woman and the Royal Chef made eyes at each other all dinner long, one place down from the hen and the College Dean. Thunder Wing sat at the end of the table, keeping an eye on Billina's peeping brood of chicks.

The Royal Chef had been able to clean and press Ozma's finest linens and the Palace Washer Woman's stew was a smash hit. As the dinner progressed, Ozma questioned each of the dinner guests closely about every single thing that Shady had done since arriving in Oz. By the time the meal was over, Ozma had a good idea of all that had happened that tumultuous day.

When the last plate was cleared, Ozma raised her hand for silence. "My friends," she said, "I have listened to each and every one of you and I have decided how to deal with Shady, Avenger of the Nome King. Come with me to my Council Chamber and we will confront him.

Everyone rose from the table and filed out of the banquet hall. Ozma led the way to her Council Chamber. Once there, they all grouped themselves around the box that held Shady captive.

Using his axe, the Tin Woodman removed the lid from the box.

"Shady," said Ozma, "the time has come for me to pass judgment on you."

Cautiously, Shady flowed up out of the box and perched on its edge.

"You have inconvenienced me, but you have done me no great harm," said Ozma, "so I will not punish you severely on my own behalf. However, you have terrified and mistreated a defenseless little bird, and if she will not forgive you, then I

The Nome King's Shadow in Oz

must punish you for that."

Ozma turned to where Billina stood with Thunder Wing and all her chicks. A light frown creased Ozma's dainty face for a moment as she tried to pick little Dorothy out from the peeping throng.

"Please step forward, little Dorothy," she said.

Dorothy stepped out of the group and looked up at the Princess.

"Little Dorothy, do you forgive this creature for taking advantage of you, scaring you and making you misbehave?"

Dorothy cocked her head at Shady. For a long moment she did not say a word.

Billina clucked and was about to answer for her little chick, but Ozma held up her hand.

"Although your bravery and quick thinking have helped save the day, Billina, you must let the little one speak for herself," said the Princess. "Otherwise, despite all your motherly love, you will be no better than Shady, making those littler than you do what *you* want."

Billina fluffed out her feathers but said nothing. Dorothy stepped out from under her mother's wing.

"Do you promise never to take advantage of

anyone else again, for as long as you live?" she asked in a solemn, piping voice.

"Yes," said Shady. "I promise."

"Then I forgive you," said Dorothy.

"Cowardly Lion?" asked Ozma, turning to the big cat.

"If the little one can forgive you," said the Cowardly Lion, "Then I can forgive you, too."

After that, the Tin Woodman and Jack Pumpkinhead forgave Shady.

"What about the Palace Washer Woman and the Royal Chef?" clucked Billina, who was still fluffing her feathers. "What about my friend, Thunder Wing?"

The Palace Washer Woman and the Royal Chef were standing there arm in arm, staring into each other's eyes.

"Shady," said the Royal Chef, dreamily. "You wrecked my greatest creation ever, but no matter. I shall bake another one. And that cake shall be my wedding cake. The Palace Washer Woman and I are going to be married, and we probably never would have come to know each other if it wasn't for you!"

The Palace Washer Woman sighed.

"Since these two have forgiven you," said Ozma.

"All that remains is for Thunder Wing to forgive you."

"Of course I forgive you," said the hawk. He looked at the Dorothys and Daniels who were still swarming over him. "If I had not come here I never would have found out what a pleasure it is to be a father. When my wing heals and I return home, I will marry the lady hawk I have been courting and start a family right away. By coming here I have learned what will truly make me happy."

"Then," said Ozma, "it is done. What do you have to say for yourself now?"

"I'm stunned," said Shady in a small voice. "In the land of the Nomes, all anyone ever does is bicker and try to get the best of each other. Here, you unite with ferocity against an enemy but you never lose your love for each other and are always ready to forgive — even your enemies. I never dreamed that this was possible. I am sorry for what I have done but I do not regret it. If I had not been so determined to seek revenge I never would have come here and learned what I now know.

"I began my life as an extension of the Nome King. Now that I am not attached to him any longer, I can learn how to be a different person. Princess Ozma, nothing would make me happier than to stay here in your Council Chamber and listen to you speak your words of kind wisdom as you rule the marvelous land of Oz. I hope that in time I will learn to be as kind, gentle and forgiving as you."

"If that is what you wish," said Ozma, "So it shall be."

"Billina," said Shady, "To make amends for the harm I have done you and your daughter, I shall change my name. From now on, I shall be called Shadow Daniel and I shall consider myself one of your sons, whether you will have me or not."

Billina dropped her head and clucked at her chicks to leave Thunder Wing alone. They ignored her.

"Oh, I think I can manage," said Billina, looking back at Shadow Daniel. "After all, you won't be eating any of my corn!"

All the people gathered there laughed and applauded. Then, they went right back to celebrating another exciting day in Oz. Their celebrations lasted long into the night.

THE END

OZ
from
Emerald City Press™

Exciting Oz Stories
from a New Generation of Authors and Artists

Adventures Under the Sea!

L. Frank Baum is best known as the author of **The Wonderful Wizard of Oz** (1900) and its thirteen sequels. Baum's other fantasies, though less well known, are equally marvelous. **The Sea Fairies**, first published in 1911, has all the magic excitement and fun for which Baum is so famous.

The Sea Fairies introduces us to Trot and Cap'n Bill, who appear in later Oz books. Their high-spirited adventures in the underwater kingdom of the Mermaids are captured in the numerous illustrations of Oz artist, John R. Neill.

Filled with fanciful characters and a touch of high adventure, **The Sea Fairies** is sure to delight the legion of fans who already love **The Wizard of Oz!**

An Underwater Classic!

Adventures High in the Sky!

L. Frank Baum, creator of Oz — America's favorite wonderland, wrote 14 fabulous tales set in that far-off fairyland. Baum's other fantasies, though less well-known, are equally marvelous. **The Sea Fairies** (1911) and its sequel, **Sky Island** (1912), are packed with the fantasy, humor and fun for which Baum is so justly famous.

Sky Island continues the adventures of young Trot and ol' Cap'n Bill, who also appear in later Oz books. Here their delightful escapades also feature favorite Oz characters Button Bright and Polychrome, the Rainbow's Daughter. As in the Oz books, John R. Neill's numerous pen-and-ink drawings capture all the excitement and joy of this wonderous tale.

Soaring on boundless imagination and filled with breathtaking adventures, **Sky Island** is sure to delight the legions of fans who already love **The Wizard of Oz.**

A High-Flying Classic!

Classic Oz Tales
from
Books of Wonder®

The Sea Fairies
by L. Frank Baum
Illustrated by John R. Neill

Sky Island
by L. Frank Baum
Illustrated by John R. Neill

Dot and Tot of Merryland
by L. Frank Baum
Newly Illustrated by
Donald Abbott

Merry Go Round in Oz
by Eloise Jarvis McGraw
and Lauren McGraw
Illustrated by Dick Martin

Captain Salt in Oz
by Ruth Plumly Thompson
Illustrated by John R. Neill

Handy Mandy in Oz
by Ruth Plumly Thompson
Illustrated by John R. Neill

The Silver Princess in Oz
by Ruth Plumly Thompson
Illustrated by John R. Neill

Ozoplaning with the Wizard
by Ruth Plumly Thompson
Illustrated by John R. Neill

The Wonder City of Oz
Written and Illustrated by
John R. Neill

The Scalawagons of Oz
Written and Illustrated by
John R. Neill

Lucky Bucky in Oz
Written and Illustrated by
John R. Neill

The Runaway in Oz
by John R. Neill
Illustrated by Eric Shanower

The Magical Mimics in Oz
by Jack Snow
Illustrated by Frank Kramer

The Shaggy Man of Oz
by Jack Snow
Illustrated by Frank Kramer

If you enjoy the Oz books and want to know more about Oz, you may be interested in **The Royal Club of Oz**. Devoted to America's favorite fairyland, it is a club for everyone who loves the Oz books. For free information, please send a first-class stamp to:

The Royal Club of Oz
P.O. Box 714
New York, New York 10011

Or call toll-free: (800) 207-6968